dabble lab

HANDS-ON PROJECTS FOR BEGINNERS

BUILDING PROJECTS

FOR BEGINNERS

TAMMY ENZ

10582827

00000430530

Raintree is an imprint of Capstone Global Library Limited, a
company incorporated in England and Wales having its registered office at Meridian
House, Sandy Lane West, Littlemore, Oxford, OX4 6LB – Registered company number:
6695582

www.raintree.co.uk
myorders@raintree.co.uk

Text © Capstone Global Library Limited 2018
The moral rights of the proprietor have been asserted.

All rights reserved. No part of this publication may be reproduced in any form or by
any means (including photocopying or storing it in any medium by electronic means
and whether or not transiently or incidentally to some other use of this publication)
without the written permission of the copyright owner, except in accordance with the
provisions of the Copyright, Designs and Patents Act 1988 or under the terms of a
licence issued by the Copyright Licensing Agency, Saffron House, 6–10 Kirby Street,
London EC1N 8TS (www.cla.co.uk). Applications for the copyright owner's written
permission should be addressed to the publisher.

ISBN 978 1 4747 5187 2 (hardback)
21 20 19 18 17
10 9 8 7 6 5 3 2 1

ISBN 978 1 4747 5191 9 (paperback)
22 21 20 19
10 9 8 7 6 5 3 2 1

• • • • • •

EDITOR
Mari Bolte

DESIGNER
Tracy McCabe

STUDIO PROJECT PRODUCTION
Marcy Morin, Sarah Schuette

PRODUCTION
Katy LaVigne

• • • • • •

Northamptonshire Libraries & Information Service CC	
Askews & Holts	

Printed and bound in India.
British Library Cataloguing in Publication Data
A full catalogue record for this book is available from the British Library.

Acknowledgements
We would like to thank the following for permission to reproduce photographs:
All photographs by Capstone Studio: Karon Dubke except Shutterstock: Gavran333,
cover (cans), Stephen Orsillo, cover (craft sticks); Illustrations by Dario Brizuela

Design Elements
Shutterstock: Alhovik, TairA

CONTENTS

BUILD IT BIGGER

How does a pile of bricks and some cement become a house? A builder with a plan knows how to take these simple things and make them into something useful. You can be a builder too.

Look around – building materials and supplies are all around you. Gather them up, and collect the tools you need. Then follow a plan and start building! You can create things that move, fly, race, play a tune and more.

Find your supplies before getting to work. You can build lots of projects with a few easy-to-find items. Collect materials and tools as you find them. They'll be waiting when you're ready to start construction.

MATERIALS:

paper, colourful card and tissue paper
paper clips, safety pins and elastic bands
thread and wire
magnets and marbles
cardboard boxes
paper towel and toilet paper tubes
syringes and tubing
paint and paint brushes
wooden craft sticks, wooden skewers and toothpicks/cocktail sticks
small pompoms
drinking straws
metal washers
empty, clean tins and disposable cups

TOOLS:

scissors
a ruler
tape
glue gun and glue sticks
marker pens and pencils

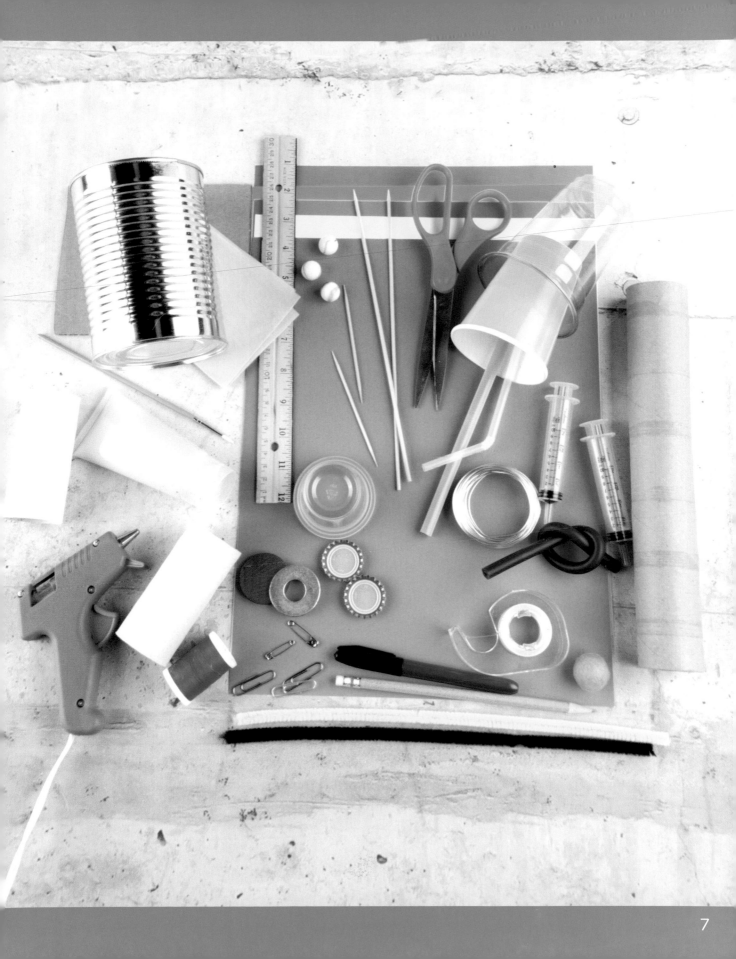

TRIANGLE BUILDING
BLOCK TOWER

Builders use steel and concrete to make the tallest towers. But did you know that card can make a great tower too? Use the same ideas and principles builders use to make a colourful paper structure.

YOU'LL NEED:

ruler
pencil
scissors
card in different colours
glue gun and glue sticks

STEPS:

1: Measure, mark and cut several 4.5-centimetre (1.75-inch)-wide card strips.

2: Measure and mark 2.5 centimetres (1 inch) from the end of one strip along one edge.

3: Connect this mark to the corner on the other edge of the strip. This will make a diagonal line. Use the ruler as a straight edge.

4: Measure and make a mark 5 centimetres (2 inches) from this corner. Connect the two marks with another diagonal line. You have made a triangle with 5-centimetre sides.

continued

5: Keep measuring and making marks every 5 centimetres along each edge of the strip.

6: Join the marks to make a series of triangles.

7: Cut the triangles apart.

8: Make 10 to 15 triangles from each colour of card.

9: Cut a 2-centimetre (.75-inch)-long slit into one of the points of each triangle.

10: Start building! Use the slits to connect two triangles.

11: Glue the triangles in place.

12: Keep adding triangles. Make the tower taller and wider.

TIP: Connect several pieces before gluing to make sure you like how it looks. Use a low-heat glue gun for safety.

WHY IT WORKS: You can build the tower as tall as you like. But the taller you go, the wider you need to build the bottom. The bottom of the tower carries more weight than the top. A wider base spreads out the weight each piece needs to support. In theory, you could build a tower as tall as you wanted - as long as the base grew at the same rate. How high can your tower go before toppling over?

PET DANCING
BUMBLEBEE

Having a pet insect might be fun. But having a pet insect that spins and flies (but doesn't sting) might be better! Build this bumblebee and use magnetic force to make it dance.

YOU'LL NEED:

2.5-by-5-centimetre (1-by-2-inch) piece of tissue paper
metal paper clip
2 pipe cleaners (one yellow and one black)
scissors
black marker pen
76-centimetre (30-inch)-long piece of thread
magnet

STEPS:

1: Gather the tissue paper in the middle.

2: Slide the tissue paper through the small loop in the paper clip. This will make the bee's wings.

3: Twist the pipe cleaners together.

4: Wrap the pipe cleaners around the paper clip. This will make a striped bumblebee body. Leave one end of the paper clip uncovered.

5: Cut off any extra pipe cleaner.

6: Use the marker to draw on eyes.

7: Tie one end of the string to the end of the paper clip.

8: Tie or tape the other end of the thread to a door handle or table edge.

9: Hold the magnet beneath the bee. Slowly move it back and forth. The bee will move too!

TIP: Hold the magnet just close enough to feel it pull on the paper clip. Try not to let the magnet and the paper clip touch.

WHY IT WORKS: The space around a magnet is called a magnetic field. When objects with iron - such as paper clips - enter the magnetic field, the field's force pulls the metal towards it. The string holds the metal paper clip away from the magnet. This allows the strong magnetic force to pull at, but not attach to, the paper clip.

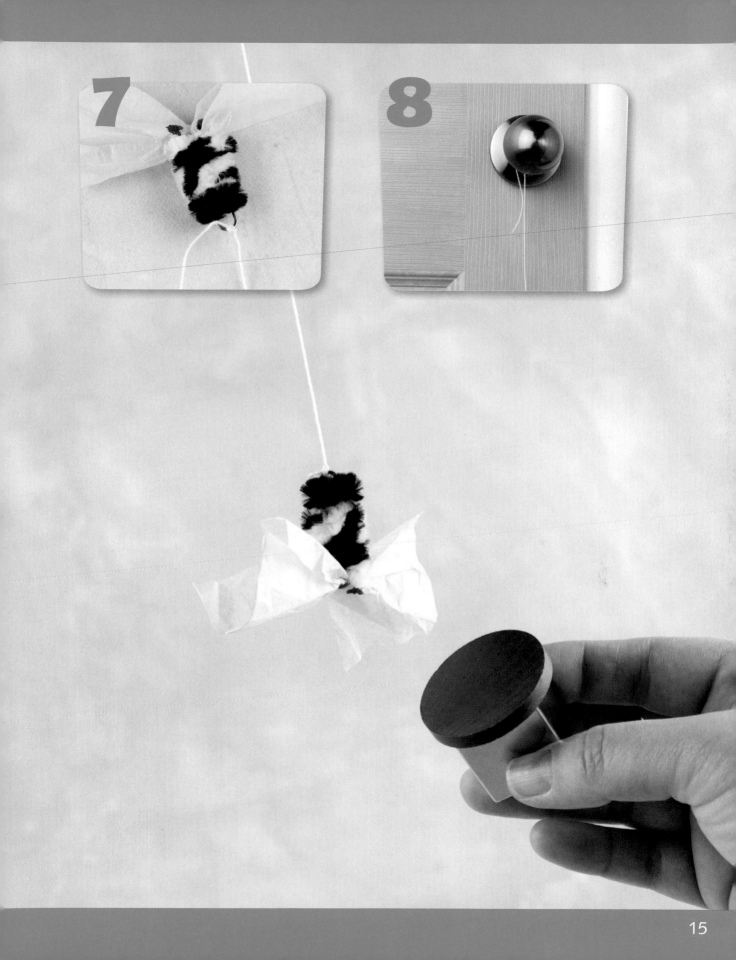

MARBLE RUN

Ready, get set, go! Get a grip on gravity with this STEAM-powered marble run. Challenge yourself to set up a run that keeps the marble going for as long as possible.

YOU'LL NEED:

scissors
5-10 toilet paper or paper towel tubes
large shallow cardboard box
tape
marble
glue gun and glue sticks

STEPS:

1: Cut each of the tubes in half across their length. These will make paths for your marbles.

2: Stand the box on its edge.

3: Tape one edge of a path near the top of the box. Make the path slope gently downwards.

4: Test the path by letting the marble roll down it.

5: Tape another path below the first, sloping in the opposite direction.

TIP: Ask an adult to help you when using sharp scissors.

6: Continue taping and testing the paths until you reach the bottom of the box. Make sure the marble stays on the track.

7: When you are sure your marble run works, remove the tape and glue the paths in place.

8: Add a small piece of a halved tube to the bottom to catch the marbles.

TIP: Challenge your friends! Who can make the fastest marble run while still using a set amount of path pieces? Who can make the slowest? What happens when you slope some paths uphill? How steep can you make them before the marble loses speed and falls backwards?

Ask an adult to help you cut a small hole at the top of the box. Then everyone will have a fair start.

WHY IT WORKS: Gravity pulls everything downwards. The marble run slows gravity's effect. It makes the marble roll back and forth, rather than straight down. Friction slows down objects as they rub against each other. When your marble has to roll uphill, the increased friction slows - or even stops - its progress. Smooth objects create less friction. Try adding texture to your tubes with materials such as paper towels or rough fabric. Record how much your marble run's time changes.

MAGIC HYDRAULIC TREASURE CHEST

There's nothing more mysterious than finding an old treasure chest. There's no need to look for a key with this chest - you can make it open on command! The lid will open and close like magic with a hidden hydraulic hinge.

YOU'LL NEED:

2 syringes

30-centimetre (12-inch)-long plastic hose with a 3-millimetre (1/8-inch) inside diameter

shoebox with a hinged lid

sharp scissors

15-centimetre (6-inch)-long piece of wire

paint and decorations (optional)

STEPS:

1: Insert each of the syringe tips into the ends of the hose.

2: Remove one of the syringe's plungers. Close the other syringe's plunger.

3: Fill the empty syringe with water. Then pull the other syringe's plunger to fill the hose and syringe with water.

4: Place the plunger back into the empty syringe. Adjust the syringes so that as one opens the other closes.

continued

5: Use the scissors to poke a small hole in the box. Make it on the back of the box, near the bottom.

6: Carefully remove one syringe from the hose. Thread the hose through the hole. Then reattach the syringe.

7: Stand the inside syringe up so its closed plunger touches the lid.

8: Poke two holes in the box, on either side of the syringe. Thread wire through the holes. Twist the ends together to hold the syringe in place.

9: Open and close the box by pushing and pulling the plunger on the syringe outside the box.

10: Paint and decorate the box to look like a treasure chest. Fill it with "treasure".

TIP: Try placing a glove on a spring inside the box. The spring will make the glove pop out when the box opens. Use it to scare your friends!

WHY IT WORKS: Hydraulics are used in many machines, such as car jacks, lifts and power drills. Hydraulics use the pressure of liquid to make things move. That pressure makes it possible to move or lift heavy objects.

MINI GOLF COURSE

Golf is a game for sunny days. But when the weather isn't nice, you can still play. This mini golf course is a great rainy-day activity. Build it from things you find around the house.

YOU'LL NEED:

green paint and paintbrush
large shallow cardboard box
scissors
3 toilet paper tubes
ruler
glue gun and glue sticks
paper
marker pen
toothpicks or cocktail sticks
jumbo craft stick
small pom-pom

STEPS:

1: Paint the inside of the box. Let the paint dry completely.

2: Use the scissors to cut the toilet paper tubes into 2.5-centimetre (1-inch) slices. Flatten slightly.

3: Cut completely through each slice. Shape the slices back into circles.

4: Arrange nine of the slices in the box. Their gaps should face in different directions. These are the holes for your golf course.

5: Use the glue gun to stick holes in place.

6: Cut nine small flags from the paper. Write a number from 1-9 on each of them.

7: Glue each flag to a toothpick. Glue each toothpick to a hole.

8: Use the craft stick as a club and the pom-pom as a ball. Hit the ball from hole to hole. Try to complete the course in as few strokes as possible.

TIP: Challenge a friend to a game. Try to keep your ball from knocking your friend's aside.

WHY IT WORKS: Sometimes small or even invisible changes in a course affect how a ball travels. Adding long grass or sand will place more friction on a ball as it rolls. Friction is a force created when objects rub against each other. That force will slow down the ball. Adding a hill to your course could speed or slow a ball, depending on its direction. Why? Gravity pulls objects towards Earth's centre.

MAGNETIC RACING TRACK

Racing car driving is a sport of speed. Bring it indoors and use the power of magnets to travel over this track.

YOU'LL NEED:

black and white paint and paintbrushes
large sheet of white card
marker pen
8 paper cups
glue gun and glue sticks
2 metal bottle tops
2 magnets

STEPS:

1: Paint a 10-centmetre (4-inch)-wide track on the card. Start the course at one edge of the board. End it on another. The course in between should curve and twist.

2: Add a white dashed line down the middle of the track to divide the lanes.

3: Label the start and finish lines with the marker pen.

4: When the paint has dried, turn the card over. Place cups on each corner of the card. Centre more cups along each edge of the board.

5: Attach all the cups to the card using the glue gun.

Start

Finish

6: When the glue is dry, turn the card back over. Place the bottle caps in separate lanes at the start line. These are the racing cars.

7: Each player gets a magnet and sits on opposite sides of the board.

8: Place the magnets under the board, beneath your car. As you drag the magnet, your car will follow.

9: Race the cars on the track. Try not to let them go off the track or out of control.

TIP: Paint or mark the bottle caps to make them look different. You can make a whole collection of cars.

WHY IT WORKS: A magnet's magnetic field pulls items towards it even when there are objects in the way. This allows you to use the magnet under the track to move the car.

Try using other magnetic objects as racing cars. Paper clips, metal toys and hardware such as nuts, screws or nails would work too. Does using a different item change how fast your car can move?

What happens when you move the magnet too quickly or turn the car too much? Test your magnet car to find out.

TIN CAN DRUM KIT

Some say it's music - others say it's a racket! Build this instrument, and you can make your own decision. Test out different tones on different tin cans. Make a noise that's all you.

YOU'LL NEED:

ruler
pencil
cardboard cereal box
scissors
drinking straw
3 jumbo craft sticks
glue gun and glue sticks
3 metal washers
wooden skewer
3 empty tin cans (different sizes)

STEPS:

1: Measure and mark a line 13 centimetres (5 inches) from the bottom of the cereal box. Do this for both the front and back.

2: Turn the box to work with the sides. Measure and mark a line 20 centimetres (8 inches) from the bottom of the box.

3: Carefully cut along these lines. Remove the top of the box.

4: Cut three 4-centimetre (1.5-inch) sections from the straw.

5: Place a craft stick across a straw piece. It should be about 5 centimetres (2 inches) from the end of the stick. Glue the stick and straw together.

6: Glue a washer to the other ends of each stick.

7: Ask an adult to poke holes in the sides of the box, about 2.5 centimetres (1 inch) from the top.

8: Slide the skewer through one of these holes. Thread the straws attached to the craft sticks onto the skewer.

9: Slide the skewer through the hole on the other side of the box.

10: Place an upside-down can under each of the washers.

11: Tap the short ends of the sticks to create a tune.

TIP: Experiment with different sized cans or drinking glasses to make different sounds.

WHY IT WORKS: Like an actual drum kit, different materials and different sized drums make a variety of sounds when played. Drums with tighter tops make higher pitches. Looser tops make lower notes. The amount of air inside the drum makes a difference, too. Smaller drums make higher notes. Larger drums create lower pitches. Sometimes the spot the drum is hit will change the sound as well.

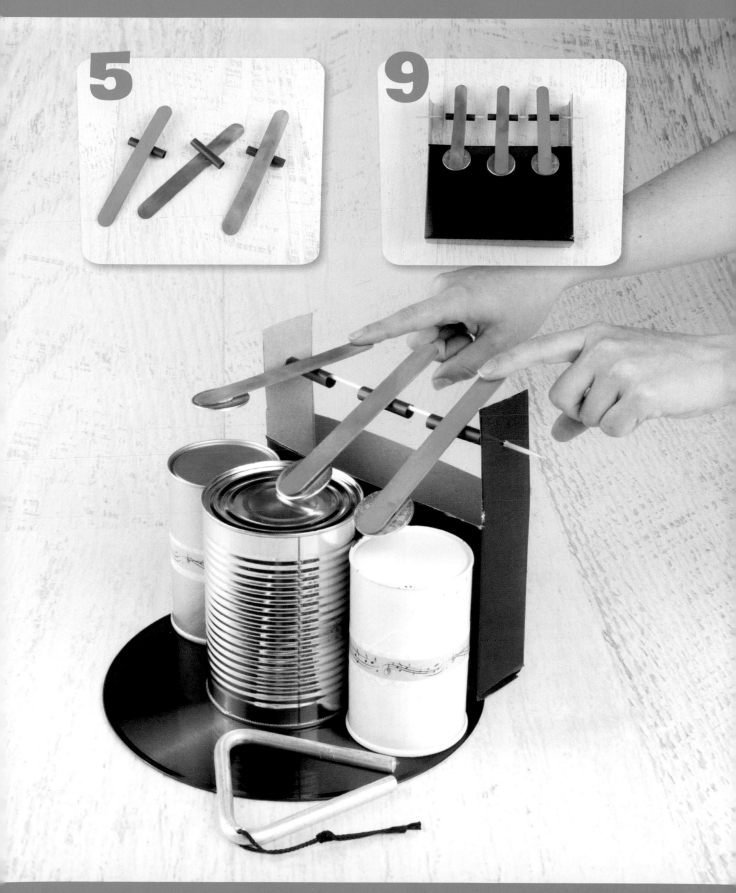

PAPER BALL
LAUNCHER

Cannons and catapults used stored energy to fire things like cannonballs and stones over long distances. Make your own cannon with elastic bands and a plastic cup. Ready, aim, fire! (Just never at anyone else!)

YOU'LL NEED:

sharp scissors

disposable paper or plastic cup

large metal paper clip

3 elastic bands

different types of ammunition (such as crumpled up paper ball, ping pong ball, or a mini tennis ball)

tape measure

STEPS:

1: Use the scissors to poke a small hole in the bottom of the cup.

2: Straighten the paper clip. Only the paper clip's small hook should remain.

3: Wrap an elastic band around the outside of the cup, near its top.

4: Slide an elastic band under the first elastic band. Pull it through itself to make a knot. Then pull it across the mouth of the cup. Give it a twist. Loop it around the bottom of the cup to hold it in place.

continued

5: Repeat step 4 with another elastic band. The elastic bands across the mouth of the cup should make an X shape.

6: Drop the paper clip into the cup. Poke the straight end through the cup's hole.

7: Bend the straight end of the paper clip. This will stop it from pulling back into the cup.

8: Loop the paper clip hook to the centre of the X.

9: Crumple the paper into a tight ball.

10: Pull on the paper clip at the bottom of the cup. This will stretch the elastic bands inwards.

11: Place the paper ball in the cup. Release the paper clip to launch the ball. Record the distance.

12: Repeat step 11 with the different types of ammunition. Compare how far each type flies.

13: Change the angle of the cannon as you shoot. Re-test and measure how far all the different types of ammunition fly.

TIP: Wrap the piece of paper clip that sticks out with tape. This will help keep the noise levels down.

WHY IT WORKS: Stretched elastic bands store energy. Used here, that energy is what launches the ammunition. When you release the paper clip, the energy in the elastic bands is transferred to the ammo. What happens when you use thicker elastic bands? What happens when you use several elastic bands rather than just one? Does the distance your ammo fly change?

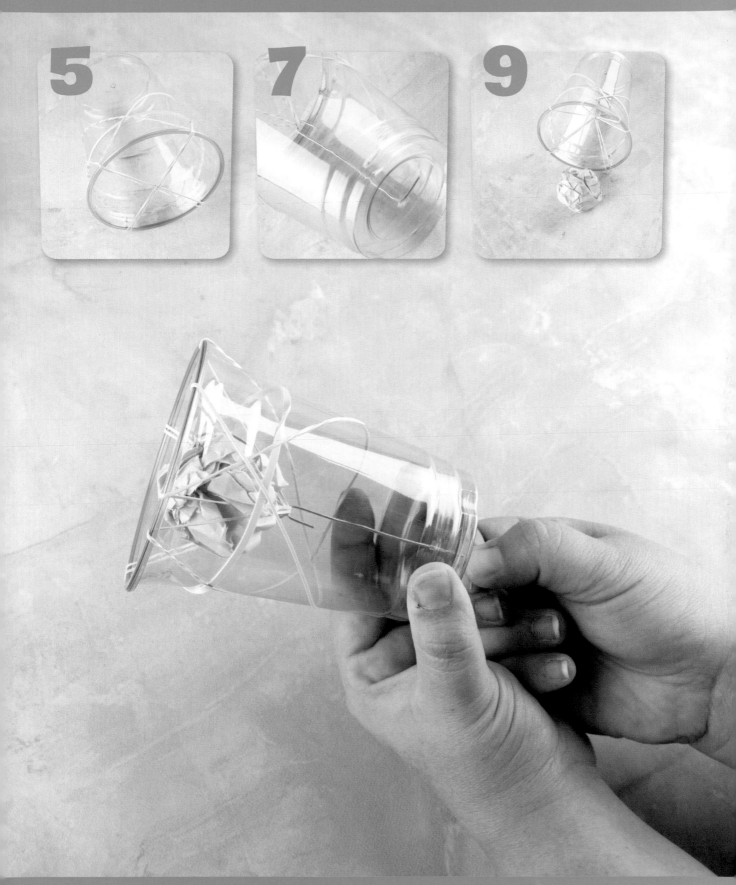

RUBE GOLDBERG
DOMINO TRIPPER

A Rube Goldberg machine uses a number of crazy steps to complete a simple goal. With this series of simple machines, you can trip a line of dominoes. You'll use a marble, a ramp and a see-saw to trip the domino run.

YOU'LL NEED:

4 bendable drinking straws
2 safety pins
scissors
tape
30 by 30-centimetre (12 by 12-inch) piece of cardboard
jumbo craft stick
wooden skewer
3 mini disposable drinking cups
glue gun and glue sticks
marble
dominoes

STEPS:

1: Make the marble ramp first. Lay three straws next to each other. Stick a safety pin through the long ends of the straws. Then clip it shut.

2: Bend the middle straw at a 90-degree angle. It will become a support for the marble ramp. Bend the other two straws slightly. These will be the ramp.

3: Cut 5 centimetres (2 inches) off of the long end of another straw.

4: Pin the short end of this straw to the short ends of the ramp.

5: Bend the bottoms of the ramp supports pieces. Tape them to the cardboard. Place the ramp to one side.

6: To make the see-saw, use the leftover piece of straw from step 3. Glue the straw to a craft stick. Place it about 2.5 centimetres (1 inch) from the end of the stick.

7: Run the skewer through the straw.

8: Place two cups upside down. Place the skewer ends on top of the cups. Glue them into place.

9: Glue the bottom of a cup to the craft stick. The cup should be on the stick's shorter side.

TIP: It might take more than one attempt to line up each part.

5

6

9

10: Place the marble ramp near the upright cup. Make sure they line up. Roll the marble down the ramp. It should land in the cup, and cause the see-saw to tip.

11: Once everything is in place, put a domino on the see-saw. It should be on the side opposite to the ramp.

12: Line up the other dominoes on the floor. Make sure they're close enough to touch when they fall.

13: Roll the marble down the ramp to set off the chain reaction to tip the line of dominoes.

WHY IT WORKS: Rube Goldberg was an American cartoonist and inventor. His drawings inspire people to create clever, over-the-top machines to perform simple tasks. This project challenges you to trip a line of dominoes. But instead of simply knocking a domino over with your finger, the machine moves a marble down a ramp and into a cup. The cup then tips a see-saw, which knocks down the dominoes. Think about other simple machines you could add to your machine, such as pulleys, levers or inclined planes. Then think about other tasks your machine could perform. Have it push a ball, make a sound or pop a balloon.

MAKE ANOTHER RUBE GOLDBERG MACHINE WITH ANY OF THESE OBJECTS!

GLOSSARY

energy ability to do work, such as moving things or giving heat or light

friction force produced when two objects rub against each other; friction slows down objects

gravity force that pulls objects together

hydraulic having to do with a system powered by fluid forced through pipes or chambers

magnetic field area of moving electrical currents that affects other objects

pitch highness or lowness of a sound; low pitches have low frequencies and high pitches have high frequencies

simple machine tool with one or no moving parts that moves an object when you push or pull

syringe tube with a plunger and a hollow needle

FIND OUT MORE

BOOKS

Awesome Craft Stick Science (Recycled Science), Jodi Wheeler-Toppen (Raintree, 2016)

Bit By Bit: Projects for Your Odds and Ends (Creative Crafts), Mari Bolte (Raintree, 2017)

Simple Machines Anne Giulieri (Raintree, 2017)

WEBSITES

www.dkfindout.com/uk/science/simple-machines/
Find out more about simple machines and how they have been used throughout history.

www.tate.org.uk/kids/make/sculpture/make-criss-cross-artwork
Build your own criss-cross masterpiece inspired by famous artists.

INDEX